Emma picked the purple toe shoes off the floor and ran her fingers along their smooth surface. Her father was coming especially to see her dance!

Her daydream was coming true. Her parents would be standing in the doorway of Miss Claudine's and they would be watching proudly as Emma danced on her toes, the center of attention.

It was a wonderful fantasy, but there was just one problem. One huge problem. Emma couldn't dance on pointe. In fact, the way her feet felt, she didn't know if she could dance at all.

Now what do I do? Emma asked herself. She could just admit defeat. Who would really care? Her mother and father, that's who. They'd say they understood, but Emma didn't want to let them down. It felt too good to have them praising her and paying attention to her. The thought of going back to being plain old Emma, lost in the shuffle of their busy lives, was too depressing.

No, there was no choice. She simply had to master the toe shoes . . . .

Other Books in the **NO WAY BALLET** series:

No Way Ballet

POINTING TOWARD TROUBLE

Suzanne Weyn

Illustrated by Joel Iskowitz

Troll Associates

Library of Congress Cataloging-in-Publication Data

Weyn, Suzanne.
  Pointing toward trouble / by Suzanne Weyn; illustrated by Joel
Iskowitz.
      p.   cm.—(No way ballet; #5)
  Summary: Hoping to impress an older ballet student and gain the
attention of her busy parents, eleven-year-old Emma lies about her
ability to dance on pointe.
  ISBN 0-8167-1653-6 (lib. bdg.)   ISBN 0-8167-1654-4 (pbk.)
  [1. Ballet dancing—Fiction.   2. Parent and child—Fiction.]
I. Iskowitz, Joel, ill.   II. Title.   III. Series: Weyn, Suzanne. No
way ballet; #5.
PZ7.W539Po   1990
[Fic]—dc20   89-34549

A TROLL BOOK, published by Troll Associates,
Mahwah, NJ 07430

Printed in the United States of America.

10   9   8   7   6   5   4   3   2   1

Chapter One

"Not this again!" Emma whispered.

"Yep. Like it or not, here she comes," said Lindsey.

"And this time she's wearing a costume," added Charlie in a disgusted voice.

The girls were slumped against the practice barre of Miss Claudine's School of Ballet. In the middle of the mirrored studio stood Miss Claudine's star pupil, Danielle Sainte-Marie. Twelve-year-old Danielle was older and taller than the other ten- and eleven-year-olds in the beginners' class. "I'm really in intermediate," she constantly reminded everyone. "I just come early to help Miss Claudine."

Today Danielle was once again demonstrating her ability to dance on her toes—or on pointe as Miss Claudine called it. Although dancers were usually older when they learned to dance on pointe, Danielle's ballet was quite advanced. Besides, she would soon be thirteen, the average age to begin pointe.

Miss Claudine had ended the last three classes with demonstrations by Danielle. The tall, dark-haired girl was now moving diagonally across the room, stand-

1

ing on the tips of her pink satin toe shoes. Her arms were held out in a wide circle in front of her, and her head was tossed back proudly. She'd costumed herself in a white tutu and thrown a feathered boa around her shoulders for dramatic effect.

"You have to admit she *is* good," said Charlie, absently twirling a piece of her chin-length red hair.

"She's not so hot," grumbled Emma.

How can she keep herself up on her toes like that? Lindsey wondered. *That must kill your feet.*

Emma began braiding the hair of her long, dark ponytail. She couldn't stand to watch Danielle any more. The whole class found Danielle's know-it-all ways annoying, but Emma disliked her even more than the others. The two girls had exchanged nothing but insults ever since the day Emma, Lindsey, and Charlie had joined the beginners' class at Miss Claudine's.

"*Très bien,* Mademoiselle Danielle!" exclaimed Miss Claudine, applauding as she joined Danielle in the center of the studio. "You improve daily."

"Thank you, Miss Claudine," crooned Danielle in the singsong voice she always used when talking to her teacher.

Yuck, thought Emma. She couldn't understand why Miss Claudine was so nice to Danielle. Miss Claudine couldn't possibly like her. The girl always had her nose stuck up in the air. And surely Miss Claudine couldn't like the way Danielle followed her around, always trying to butter her up.

But, Emma reasoned, Miss Claudine was nice to everyone. She'd been nice to Emma, Charlie, and

Lindsey, even though, at first, the three girls had made their dislike for ballet pretty clear. They'd done a lot of things which would have made any other teacher furious. They'd sneaked out of class, gotten lost on a field trip, and generally goofed around enough to drive a less patient person insane.

Miss Claudine, however, took it all in stride. She'd push back her ash-blond hair and say something like, "Each girl must blossom in her own time, *chérie,*" or, "Either one loves the ballet, or one does not. There is no forcing the issue."

Miss Claudine's patience and love of ballet had slowly won over the three girls. Even Emma—who really hated ballet at first—was beginning to enjoy class.

But she did not enjoy seeing Danielle Sainte-Marie twice a week!

Miss Claudine's musical voice cut through Emma's thoughts. " . . . and so, you see that though dancing on pointe is not easy, it is very beautiful. I've had Danielle demonstrate so that you could all see what there is to look forward to, and how much hard work is to be done before each of you buys her first pair of toe shoes."

Danielle raised her nose just a little higher as Miss Claudine spoke. "Now, mademoiselle," said Miss Claudine to Danielle, "let us show the class the supported arabesque on pointe, which you've just learned. I will be your partner."

Looking nervous, Danielle let Miss Claudine support her as she lifted one leg up behind her and bent

forward. She was up on one toe for half a second and then stumbled forward.

Emma turned to Charlie and Lindsey with a satisfied grin. "See, I told you she wasn't that—" Emma began, but she was cut short by the sound of two people clapping loudly.

The girls looked toward the door and saw a heavy woman with short brown hair wearing a navy blue suit. She was still clapping and smiled brightly. The stocky, balding man beside her was also applauding. "Brava! Brava!" the man called out. Danielle looked at them and blushed, but she didn't seem to really mind their attention.

"Those are Danielle's parents," said Charlie.

"How do you know?" Lindsey asked.

"Don't you remember? Mr. Sainte-Marie drove one of the buses when we went to Lincoln Center," Charlie reminded her. "And that has to be her mother. She has the same face as Danielle, only fat."

"I would just die if my parents came and did that," said Emma.

"Me, too," Charlie agreed.

"The way we dance, I don't think our parents would ever come and start yelling brava," Lindsey said with a wry smile. She didn't have to remind them that they were the worst dancers in the class.

Charlie giggled. "My father would probably yell, 'Give me my money back!' if he saw me try to dance on my toes."

"I don't believe this," said Emma, jerking her head toward the studio door. Danielle had joined her parents, and her father was handing her a rose. "Her father brings her a flower because she stands on her toes for half a second! How twerpy!"

"I think it's kind of nice," Lindsey disagreed.

"You're strange," said Emma, shaking her head.

"All right," Miss Claudine said, turning to face the rest of the girls. "That will be all for today. *Au revoir, chéries.*"

"Did you see the flowers Danielle's parents gave her after the recital on Eastbridge Day?" asked Charlie as the girls walked toward the dressing room. "The bouquet was humongous! Okay, she was the star of the show and all, but it was as big as she is."

"It's a pretty big deal to dance on your toes," Lindsey said. "It kind of makes you an official ballerina, I think. I could never do it, I know that."

"You could, too," Emma argued as they entered the narrow dressing room. "It's not that big a deal."

"Then how come Miss Claudine makes such a fuss over it?" asked Charlie, pulling off her baby-blue leotard.

"Because I think Danielle is the only one in the intermediate class who can do it," Emma explained. "At least that's what Danielle was telling everyone before class today. But I've seen lots of girls on pointe in other ballet classes I've taken."

"You mean in other classes you've been kicked out of," Lindsey teased with a laugh.

"Asked to withdraw from," Emma corrected, her eyes twinkling mischievously. Emma's mother had been forcing her to take ballet classes for years. Never one to be forced to do anything, Emma always managed to be such a nuisance that her teachers always

6

called Mrs. Guthrie and asked her to take Emma out of class. But Mrs. Guthrie was just as stubborn as her daughter, and she kept re-enrolling Emma in different ballet classes. She was sure Emma had a natural gift for dance. And whether Emma liked it or not, she was going to see that gift developed.

"Anyway," Emma continued, "what I'm trying to say is that Danielle may be a hotshot here, but in bigger schools nobody is all that impressed with themselves because they're on pointe. So it must not be that hard."

"For your information, it is extremely difficult."

Emma turned and saw Danielle standing in the doorway, her pink toe shoes tied together and hanging around her neck.

"Maybe it's tough for a pea brain like you, Danielle," Emma snapped.

Danielle just looked at Emma with a smug, superior expression. She went to a locker and pulled out her dance bag. "When you can dance on pointe, we'll talk about it," she said as she headed back out the door. "I'm sure that day will never come." With that, Danielle tossed her head back and swirled out of the dressing room.

"I'm sure that day will never come," Charlie mimicked in a shrill, high-pitched imitation of Danielle's voice.

"Barfo," stated Lindsey flatly. She stuck her tongue out at the spot where Danielle had stood.

Emma bent forward and furiously brushed her thick hair. She was more bugged by Danielle than ever before. The girl's high-and-mighty attitude made her see red. And now there was something more. The picture of Danielle smiling while her parents applauded had gotten stuck in Emma's head, and it was making her even angrier than Danielle's snobby remarks.

"Anyone can go on pointe," said Emma, looking up at Charlie and Lindsey. "Those shoes do most of the work for you."

"Are you sure?" asked Lindsey doubtfully. She pulled on her down jacket and quickly fluffed the blond curls of her shoulder-length hair. "Do you think you could do it?"

"Sure," said Emma, "if I had the right shoes."

When they were done dressing, the girls headed out toward the front office. Danielle and her parents were standing by Miss Claudine's big desk. Mr. Sainte-Marie had his hand on his daughter's shoulder. "Yes, if Danielle continues to work hard, she may well have a future in dance," they heard Miss Claudine tell Danielle's parents.

"We only want the best for our Danielle," Mr. Sainte-Marie said in a voice that Emma found obnoxiously loud. "She's our pride and joy."

"That she is," Mrs. Sainte-Marie agreed.

Miss Claudine smiled. "It's good to see you, but you really must excuse me. I have another class coming in."

"Certainly," said Mr. Sainte-Marie, "but just let me ask you one more question about Danielle's future as a dancer . . ."

"Poor Miss Claudine," whispered Charlie. "She can't escape Danielle's parents."

They pushed open the glass doors and walked out into the Eastbridge Mall. The dance studio was on the lower level. The girls walked up the ramp toward the upper level and the parking lot.

"Do you really think you could dance on pointe?" Charlie asked Emma.

"Definitely," Emma answered.

"Because you know what would really burn Danielle?" Charlie continued. "It would make her crazy if you could dance on pointe, too. Then she couldn't go around acting so superior all the time."

"Could you imagine Danielle's face if Emma started dancing on her toes?" said Lindsey. "She'd croak!"

Charlie's face lit up. "Do you think you could do it, Emma?"

"I don't have toe shoes."

"We could all pool our money together and get you some," Lindsey said. "They can't be that expensive."

Emma thought about it. Dancing on pointe didn't *look* that hard to do. And she was sick of watching Danielle show off. "I would love to see her face if I showed up wearing toe shoes. It would prove she wasn't queen of the universe."

"Let's do it, then," urged Charlie.

"Okay," Emma agreed. When she'd taken ballet in Manhattan, she'd seen whole classfuls of girls on pointe. The girls were older, but so what? If they could all do it, it certainly couldn't be *that* hard.

The girls walked out the back exit of the mall, where Charlie's mother, Mrs. Clark, was waiting for them in her blue hatchback. It was her turn to drive in the car pool she'd formed in order to get the girls back and forth to ballet class.

In less than twenty minutes Mrs. Clark had dropped Lindsey off and was turning up the block toward Emma's house. "See you in school tomorrow," Emma said to Charlie as she scooted out of the car.

"See you, twinkle toes," Charlie giggled.

Emma smiled and ran up the walk to her house. She fished for her house key, which was buried deep inside her tapestry handbag. She waved to Mrs. Clark when she found it and let herself into the house.

"Anybody home?" she called from the front hallway. There was no answer. Emma sighed and threw her bag on the white leather couch in the living room.

When her family had lived in Manhattan, her mother had worked part-time, so she was always there when Emma came home in the afternoon. But since the divorce, Emma's mother had begun working full-time. And after she and Emma moved out to Eastbridge, she'd started her own literary agency. Now, it seemed to Emma, she worked *all* the time. Emma often came home to an empty house.

Emma went into the kitchen and opened the refrigerator. She stared into it, looking for something appealing to eat. *Yogurt—yuck. Grapes—boring.* She spotted a doggy bag from a restaurant. *Perfect!* Emma's mother ate out a lot and the leftovers she brought home were always good.

She opened the bag. A wedge of thick chocolate cake was nestled inside. Grabbing a fork, Emma took the bag into the living room and settled down in front of their wide-screen TV.

The cake reminded Emma of the luscious desserts they served at Murphy's Restaurant near Lincoln Center. She used to eat there with her parents at least once a week. It was their favorite restaurant. The older waiters knew the Guthries and addressed Emma by name.

Popping a forkful of the chocolate into her mouth, Emma smiled as she recalled the fun they used to have. Her father would tell funny stories about the clients in his law office, and her mother would talk about the famous authors who came into the publishing house where she worked. They'd play games like making up stories about the newer waiters.

"That one is so skinny, he must be a starving artist," Mrs. Guthrie once suggested. "He probably works all day and paints all night and never has time to eat or sleep."

"And that one has such a mean expression. He's probably a lion tamer in the circus," Emma had giggled.

"He doesn't even need a whip. He just has to look at the lions and they shiver in fear," her father had laughed.

Emma shook her head sadly. They'd had so many good times together, but that felt like so long ago. Now it seemed that her parents were always busy. And the last time she'd been to Murphy's had been with her father and his dumb girlfriend, Dawn. No, the divorce had ruined everything. Even Murphy's.

She began clicking the remote control, looking for something interesting to watch, when she heard the jangle of keys in the door. "Hi, sweetie," called Mrs. Guthrie from the front hall. "How was ballet?"

"Same as usual," Emma replied as she jumped up, quickly swallowed the last bite of cake, and started picking chocolate crumbs off the white carpet.

Mrs. Guthrie came into the living room, her arms full of papers. "Can you believe all these manuscripts I have to read?" she asked, nodding at the papers. "When I decided to become an agent, I never realized the amount of reading involved. I have to read these stories before I can try to sell them to a publisher. Maybe I'll take one of those speed-reading classes!"

Emma's mother went to the phone answering machine on the glass end table and listened to her messages: the cleaning lady would be late on Saturday; a friend of hers called to say hi; a client had a question about a book he'd written. And Emma's father had called to say he wouldn't be able to pick Emma up on Sunday. "A business thing, you understand," his deep voice explained on the machine.

Mrs. Guthrie wrinkled her face apologetically at Emma. "Business," she said.

"Business," Emma repeated. She wasn't exactly surprised. Her father still lived in the city. He was supposed to see her every Sunday and on school vacations, but he often had to cancel their visits due to business.

"Your haircut looks nice," Emma said, eager to change the subject. Her mother had always worn her thick brown hair back in a tight bun, as if she really were the dancer she once dreamed of becoming. She'd just had it cut the other day in a new style that waved down to her chin.

Mrs. Guthrie stood and examined herself in the large wall mirror. "Do you really think so? I'm changing my life, so I figured I'd change my image, too. You don't think it looks too . . . too teenager-ish?"

"No, it's cool," Emma assured her.

"We look so much alike, Emma," said her mother, still examining the image of her own delicate face in the mirror. "Maybe you should have your hair cut like this."

"No, thanks," Emma said quickly. "I like my hair just the way it is."

"A short cut would bring out your eyes, though. You have such pretty eyes."

"Nope. I like long hair," Emma insisted.

Emma was enjoying chatting with her mother like this. Mrs. Guthrie was often so busy that all they did was exchange important information—like who was going to be where and when, or how much money Emma needed, or what time Emma's father was going to pick her up. They rarely just talked about everyday things like hair.

Mrs. Guthrie sat down on the floor next to Emma. Emma always liked the fact that her mother wasn't like other mothers in Eastbridge. Mrs. Guthrie seemed younger. Emma could never picture Charlie's mother settling down on the floor with them. "Nothing on the tube?" asked Mrs. Guthrie.

"Nope," Emma said, snapping off the set. She leaned back on her elbows. Back in their old apart-

ment, she and her mother had often sat on the floor together, playing board games and talking. When Emma decided board games were too babyish, they'd paged through fashion magazines together.

"You didn't learn *anything* new in ballet?" her mother questioned, casually picking a strand of hair from Emma's purple sweater.

"You know, something did happen in ballet today," Emma said. "That snobby girl, Danielle—remember the one who was the swan princess in the recital?—well, she was showing off in her new toe shoes. So Lindsey and Charlie and I decided—"

"Emma, dear, hold on a minute," her mother interrupted. "I just remembered that I have to make a phone call to a publisher in California. I can never remember, is the time there three or five hours behind us?"

"I don't know," answered Emma glumly.

"Well, I'll just be a sec." Mrs. Guthrie got up and hurried down the hall into her study. Emma rolled over onto her back and pulled a fashion magazine from the coffee table and began flipping through it.

After a while, she stood and walked up the stairs to her room in one of the newly added on dormers. She clicked on the light. *Boy, what a mess!* she thought, looking around her room. Her watercolor pens were scattered everywhere, along with the clothing sketches she'd been drawing. A pile of music cassettes was lying on the shaggy carpet next to a large heap of clothes that Emma kept meaning to bring downstairs to wash. The top of her dresser had all but disappeared under the collection of fashion magazines, costume jewelry, and school books Emma had carelessly tossed on it.

Kicking off her black felt slippers, she crawled under her zebra-striped comforter. She looked up at the ceiling and let her mind wander. Before long she was thinking about Danielle. She kept seeing the image of Danielle's parents applauding and making such a fuss over their daughter. "Dumb," she muttered.

Emma tried to remember the last time her parents had fussed over her like that. It must have been two years ago, when she'd won first place in the school art contest. That was before their divorce. Ever since then, they always seemed to be too busy to notice Emma for long. She tried to imagine them coming to class and bringing her flowers, but she couldn't.

Suddenly Emma had an uncomfortable thought. Could it be that she was jealous of Danielle and the way her parents made a big deal over everything she did?

Jealous of Danielle! The thought was revolting. Emma rolled onto her side and pulled the comforter over her head.

Chapter Two

"Lindsey, it was nice of your father to drive us," said Emma as she, Charlie, and Lindsey walked through the Eastbridge Mall.

Lindsey shrugged. "He was coming here anyway. That woman in the front seat with him is his *date*. They're going to an early movie at the triplex."

"I was wondering!" cried Charlie. "Is it serious?"

"I hope not," groaned Lindsey. "She giggles at everything my father says. It's so dumb." Lindsey knew it was a good sign that her father was finally beginning to date—it had been several years since her mother's death. She simply didn't understand his taste in women.

The girls had just left Mr. Munson and were heading to Cappel's dance wear shop on the upper level of the mall. It was supper time and the wide aisles were unusually empty. Without the crowd of people, the soft music seemed extra loud. They stopped in front of a narrow store with bright leotards displayed in the front window.

"This is so exciting," said Charlie. "I can't believe

we're actually going to buy toe shoes. Do you know what this reminds me of?"

"No," said Lindsey. "But I'll bet ten dollars it reminds you of something you saw on TV."

"How did you know?" Charlie asked, surprised.

"Everything reminds you of something on TV!" cried Emma.

"Okay, so I love TV. Big deal," said Charlie. "This reminds me of a TV movie I saw where a dancer bought toe shoes, but she didn't know that secret documents were sewn into the soles. All these foreign agents were following her all over the place."

"What happened to her?" asked Emma, her eyes wide.

"One agent finally cornered her and tried to push her down an elevator shaft, but then—"

"All right, already!" interrupted Lindsey. "That's not going to happen to Emma. The only one who might chase us would be the salesperson when she realizes we don't even know anything about toe shoes."

"Don't worry," Emma assured her. "There's nothing to know."

Lindsey looked skeptical. "I don't want to hurt your feelings or anything," she said, "but you're not exactly the greatest dancer in the class. Are you sure you should be doing this?"

Emma dropped her jaw and put her hands on her hips. "Thanks loads, Lindsey. You're supposed to be my friend."

"Come on, Emma," Lindsey cried. "You know it's true! The three of us are the worst dancers at Miss

Claudine's. I mean, we've all improved, but that's not saying much."

"Emma is the best of the three of us," Charlie pointed out.

"Big deal," Lindsey argued. "On a scale of one to ten, you and I are zeros and Emma's a one."

"You haven't been paying attention," Emma stated in a tone of injured pride. "I've been dancing much better lately. The other day I did an arabesque and didn't even fall forward the way I usually do. Besides, you know Miss Claudine says my problem is that I just don't try. Well, now I'm going to try."

"If you say so," said Lindsey doubtfully as she pushed open the glass door.

Emma, Charlie, and Lindsey entered the cluttered store. Leotards in bright colors and patterns were displayed on the walls. There were pictures from magazines showing dancers in costume tacked around the store. One wall was completely mirrored, like the studio at Miss Claudine's, and it even had a practice barre running along the mirrors.

On the other side of the store was a long glass counter covered with baskets full of gauzy hair adornments, as well as practical hair clips and headbands. Shoes were displayed inside the case. There were tap shoes and soft, flat ballet slippers like the ones Emma, Lindsey, and Charlie wore for class. There were delicate satin toe shoes, their ribbons spread out artistically around them. Behind the case, stacked high against the wall, were rows of shoeboxes.

Charlie grabbed Emma's arm and squeezed excitedly. "This is it," she whispered. "Your first pair of toe shoes. You're going to be a real ballerina."

Emma smiled back at her nervously. She felt like she had the words *fake* and *phony* written across her forehead. This was a store for people who took dancing seriously—something Emma had never done.

She pushed that thought aside. It was foolish. This store was simply there for anyone who wanted to buy what it had to sell. And today Emma fit that category. She wanted toe shoes.

A tall, slender saleswoman with long, straight, black hair stood behind the glass counter. "Can I help you, ladies?" she asked.

"Our friend here is buying her first pair of toe shoes," Charlie spoke up.

"Congratulations," said the saleswoman, smiling. "What size do you need?"

"Five," said Emma.

"Do you want five or three?" the woman asked.

The girls looked at one another. "I said size five," Emma repeated.

"What size shoe do you wear?" asked the woman.

Emma looked at her friends with an expression of disbelief. "Am I crazy or is she?" she whispered. "Didn't I say size five twice?"

Charlie and Lindsey shrugged their shoulders. "Try again," Lindsey suggested.

It occurred to Emma that maybe the woman was hard of hearing, so she tried to speak clearly. "I . . . need . . . a . . . size . . . five!" she said slowly in a very loud voice.

The saleswoman smiled. "I heard you, dear. You

20

have to buy toe shoes two sizes smaller than your regular size. If you normally take a size five shoe, then you need a size three toe shoe."

Emma could feel herself start to blush with embarrassment. "Oh," she said. "I take a size five shoe, so I guess I need a size three."

"And color?" asked the woman.

This time Emma had no doubt in her mind. "Purple," she said, naming her very favorite color.

"Are you sure you want purple shoes?" asked Lindsey, wrinkling her nose up.

"*I'm* going to wear them and that's the color I want," Emma insisted.

"I'm not sure we have threes in purple, but I'll look," said the saleswoman. She pushed a rolling ladder down to the far end of the wall and soon returned with a shoe box. "We have a lavender pair after all," she said, opening the box and handing it to Emma.

Emma looked down at the graceful shoes nestled in their tissue paper, their satin gleaming. "They're too pretty to walk in," she said.

"You don't walk in them, you dance," said the woman. She looked at Emma with a serious expression. "You seem quite young to be on pointe."

"I'm not as young as I look. I'm, um, thirteen," she said, adding two years onto her age.

"That's still young. Have you been dancing long?"

"All my life, practically since I was born," Emma lied.

"You should see her, she's amazing," Charlie chimed in, afraid that the woman wouldn't sell them the shoes if she thought Emma wasn't ready for them.

"I'm sure she is," the woman said. "Sit in that chair and slip them on. See how they feel to you."

Emma tried on the shoes. She stuck her feet straight out and wiggled them in front of her. "They're really pretty," she sighed. She leaned back in the chair and tapped her toes together as though she were leaping through the air.

"Magnificent leap," giggled Charlie.

"Brava!" Lindsey cried.

"How do they feel?" asked the saleswoman.

"They're a little stiff, but they don't hurt," Emma answered. "Do you think I need a bigger size?"

The woman knelt and gently pressed her fingers along Emma's right foot. "Your toes aren't pushing up. No, this is the size you want. Go over to the barre and see how they feel when you stand up on them."

"Uh, no thanks," said Emma. "I'm sure they're fine. I'll take them."

"How much are they?" asked Lindsey.

"These are twenty-five dollars," the woman told them, taking the shoes from Emma and putting them back in the box. "Plus tax, of course."

Lindsey and Charlie looked at one another with glum expressions. Each girl had brought her entire savings. They had enough money, but they'd been hoping they wouldn't have to spend *all* of it.

"Naturally you'll want ribbons for those," said the woman.

"Naturally," Emma agreed cheerfully. "Purple ones."

The woman took two lavender satin ribbons from a drawer behind the counter and placed them inside

the box. "The ribbons are a dollar-fifty extra. Do you need a lamb's-wool sock?"

"What's that?" asked Charlie.

"It's just a lining to protect your toes and the front of your foot."

"How much is it?" Lindsey asked quickly.

"Just another twelve dollars," the woman answered.

"She doesn't need it," snapped Charlie. She'd been hoping to save enough money to buy herself a small portable black-and-white TV for her room. Now she'd have to start saving all over again.

"I'll skip the sock," said Emma, willing to save some money on such an unglamorous item.

"Very well," said the woman, "but I think your teacher would want you to have it. The sock will help cushion you against any initial discomfort."

"Oh, she doesn't even know—" Charlie began. A sharp poke from Emma stopped her from revealing that Miss Claudine didn't know a thing about the shoes. "She doesn't know the meaning of the word discomfort," Charlie covered her mistake quickly. "She says discomfort is good."

"She does?" asked the woman, raising a skeptical eyebrow.

"Oh, yes," Lindsey assured her. "She's from, you know, the old school of ballet. The discomfort school."

"Lucky you," muttered the woman as she wrote up the sales slip. The girls placed their money on the counter. "Good-bye, new catcher's mitt," moaned Lindsey.

"Enjoy your shoes," said the woman, handing Emma her bag, "Oh, by the way, I use floor wax on my shoes. It makes them very hard. You can get as much as three or four months out of them that way."

"Thanks," chirped Emma brightly as she joined Charlie and Lindsey at the entrance. "I will."

"These only last three or four *months*!" gasped Lindsey when they were outside. "We can't afford another pair."

"Relax," said Emma. "That's for real dancers who practice every day." Emma looked at her two friends. "Stop acting so bummed out about the money," she told them. "Think about the look on Danielle's face when we knock her off her high horse. It'll be worth it."

"I guess so," said Charlie, brightening a bit. "And you know, this is only phase one of our operation."

"Would you stop talking like this is a spy movie," grumbled Lindsey.

"Okay," sighed Charlie. "I just feel this is very important and it's top secret like a spy case. And Danielle is like an enemy agent, and—"

"Charlie!" cried Lindsey, rolling her eyes impatiently. "Get to the point. Why is this only phase one?"

"Because phase two is coming up with a dance routine that will make Danielle really jealous."

"Why do we have to do that?" asked Emma. "Isn't it enough that I show up on pointe?"

"Think big, Emma!" cried Charlie, fired with enthusiasm. "You don't want to be equal to Danielle, you want to leave her in the dust. Besides, you can't just tiptoe in there in toe shoes. You have to have some reason to be on pointe. Otherwise you might not even get the chance to show Miss Claudine what you can do."

"I suppose," Emma agreed. "But how are we going to come up with a dance?"

"Leave it to me," answered Charlie confidently. "I've been thinking about this all day. I can just see it all in my head, like a movie. I'll think up a dance for us."

"Now what?" asked Emma, checking her purple plastic watch. "We have more than an hour until we meet Lindsey's father. Where do you want to go?"

The girls gazed around the mall, trying to decide where to go next. Suddenly Lindsey's eyes lit up. "Hey, look, it's Miss Claudine," she said, pointing several stores down to where their ballet teacher was window-shopping, arm in arm with her handsome blond boyfriend, Adrian.

"He's so cute," sighed Charlie. The girls knew Adrian; he had helped Miss Claudine with their recital and driven a bus on their field trip. Charlie thought he was the ultimate boyfriend. Only Mark Johnson from her fifth-grade class equaled him in cuteness as far as Charlie was concerned.

"Nice cape," added Emma, noticing Miss Claudine's calf-length red wool cape, which topped off black boots. Miss Claudine had a flare for dramatic dressing that Emma admired.

At that moment, Miss Claudine looked up and noticed them watching her. She smiled and waved. "Hello, *chéries,*" she called.

Emma quickly hid her bag behind her back as Miss Claudine and Adrian walked toward them. She knew Miss Claudine wouldn't approve of her going on pointe. She'd think Emma wasn't ready for it. Emma had to hope that once Miss Claudine saw her dance, she'd change her mind. Until then, Emma thought it best to keep the toe shoes a secret.

"And look! You are coming out of Cappel's!" said Miss Claudine, stopping to talk to them in front of the store. "What have you bought?"

"Just a new leotard," Emma answered.

"They carry everything in this store," said Adrian, who was also a dancer. "I once rented a dancing duck costume from them."

"How come?" asked Lindsey.

Adrian shook his head and chuckled. "I had a chance to be in a commercial. I thought it would be my big break, but . . . oh, never mind."

Miss Claudine kissed Adrian affectionately on the cheek. "You will be known as a great dancer, not a dancing duck," she assured him with a sweet laugh.

"Can I ask you something, Miss Claudine?" said Charlie. She glanced quickly at Emma and Lindsey, her eyes bright with an idea.

"But, of course, *chérie*. What is it?"

"If we came up with a new dance, one that we made up ourselves, could we show it to you and the class?"

"Yes, of course," said Miss Claudine. "I will give you some time at the end of class. Just tell me when you'll be ready and I'll schedule it in."

Charlie thought for a second. "A week from this Saturday. We'll be ready by then."

"I hope you won't be doing anything we haven't covered in class," Miss Claudine warned. "It can be very dangerous to try new steps on your own."

"Don't worry, Miss Claudine," said Emma. "You're going to be very impressed with this performance."

Miss Claudine studied them a moment. Though this evening she wore her hair in loose waves around her shoulders, she still smoothed the top of her hair with her hand—the same way she smoothed it when it was tied back during class. It was a sure sign that she was trying to figure something out.

The girls knew it must seem strange to her that the three biggest goof-ups in her class were suddenly hanging out at a dance wear store and planning performances on their own. But the skeptical look passed from Miss Claudine's face and she smiled at them. "I am glad to see such enthusiasm for the ballet."

"You know us, Miss Claudine," said Charlie.

"Yes," said Miss Claudine, smoothing her hair once again, "yes . . . I do."

Chapter Three

"Ouch!" cried Charlie. She sucked the dot of blood from her thumb. "I can't sew the ribbons onto these dumb shoes. The material is too hard."

"You're almost finished," Lindsey encouraged her. It was Friday afternoon, the day after their trip to Cappel's. Charlie, Emma, and Lindsey were sitting in the finished basement of Emma's house. Charlie was sewing the ribbons onto Emma's toe shoes using a large darning needle, the only needle Emma could find.

After a few minutes, Charlie held up the shoes by their ribbons. "There. All done."

"They look a little . . . a little lopsided," said Emma, studying the satin shoes. "One ribbon is sewed on toward the arch and the other ribbon is back toward the heel."

Charlie threw her hands up in the air. "Then you do it!" she cried. "I did my best."

"I can't sew," said Emma in a grouchy voice.

"Anybody can sew," scolded Charlie. "You just don't want to do it."

"Hey, cut it out," said Lindsey, taking the shoes from Charlie. "This is good enough. The ribbons will hold the shoes on your feet. That's all that matters."

"Well, I don't want them to look goofy," Emma sulked.

"They won't," Lindsey said, handing her the shoes. "Try them."

Emma was wearing her baby-blue leotard and tights. She sat back on the old brown suede couch and pulled her knees up to her chest. "How do you tie these things, anyway?" she asked, looking at the ribbons with a puzzled expression.

"Just sort of crisscross them," suggested Lindsey.

"Here, there's a picture in this book," Charlie said, fishing a large hardcover book from her bag. The book was titled *The Art of Ballet* and had a picture of a famous ballet dancer on the cover. Charlie opened to a close-up shot of a dancer's feet wearing toe shoes. "See, you just kind of wrap it all up around your ankles."

Emma studied the picture. "They look dumb like that. I think they would look better wrapped higher up my leg."

Charlie quickly flipped through the book. "I don't see that anywhere," she told Emma. "Better tie them around your ankle."

"I don't like the way it looks," Emma insisted.

"I think you'd better do it their way," Charlie urged, putting the book down on the couch next to Emma so that she could study the picture of the shoes as she tied her own. Emma sighed and imitated the picture as best she could, but somehow the result was not the same. "You must have sewed these ribbons on wrong," she grumbled.

"Here, I'll do it," said Lindsey as she knelt in front of Emma. She undid Emma's bow and retied the ribbons lower down on her ankle. The two ends still didn't meet on the side as they did in the picture. "I'll just tie them right back here. It'll be good enough," she said calmly.

When Lindsey was done, Emma studied her feet. The shoes weren't perfect—they gapped a bit under her arches, and Charlie's stitching *was* a bit sloppy— but they were close enough to the image Emma had in mind. And, Emma thought, the gorgeous light purple sheen of the shoes more than made up for any minor imperfections.

A small smile formed on Emma's lips. She pictured herself gracefully gliding across the floor of Miss Claudine's. She could just imagine Miss Claudine, her eyes wide with delighted disbelief as she watched her. And in this imagined scene she saw Danielle frowning and skulking out of the studio—thoroughly embarrassed by the superiority of Emma's dancing.

"Okay, stand up," said Lindsey. "Let's see you tiptoe around on these things."

"I didn't say I would be able to do it right away," Emma warned. "You're going to have to help me."

"We will," Charlie assured her. "That's why I took out this book from the library. It's all about great ballet dancers. I thought we could look at the pictures and figure out what to do."

Emma got up and walked around in a circle. She circled both her arms out in front of her, as if she were

THE ART OF BALLET

From ...

JULIA ELIZABETH

a great ballerina, and made a small leap across the room, landing flat on her feet. Then she kicked out her leg and twirled it in the air.

"Terrific," said Lindsey dryly, "but let's see you get up on your toes."

"Hold on," Emma said. "I'm warming up."

"You're stalling," Charlie corrected.

Emma wrinkled her nose up at Charlie. "Okay, okay. Here goes." She swung her arms forward in an effort to scoot herself up onto her toes. Nothing happened. She swung her arms again, and this time she stumbled forward.

"I have an idea," said Lindsey. "Charlie and I will get on either side of you until you're on your toes, and then we'll let go of you once you're up."

"Okay," Emma agreed. Charlie stood on one side, while Lindsey took the other. Emma stretched out her arms and let both girls support her weight with their shoulders. Pushing up, she managed to boost herself onto her toes. "Hey, this is working!" she cried happily.

"You're doing it!" Charlie encouraged her. "You're wobbling a little, but you're up."

Emma used all her concentration to stay balanced, but it wasn't easy. It felt as if all her weight was pressing down on the second toe of each foot, and almost instantly those toes began to throb with pain. Then the inside muscles of her thighs started quivering as she struggled to keep her legs straight.

"Charlie, now you let go," instructed Lindsey.

"No!" Emma cried nervously.

"We can't hold you up forever," said Lindsey. "Let go very slowly, Charlie."

Charlie slipped out from under Emma's arm. Emma teetered forward and then backward as she tried to stay balanced. She pulled in her tummy muscles in an effort to keep her backside from sticking out behind her. Then she leaned sideways, putting all her weight onto Lindsey's shoulders.

The throbbing had now spread to all her toes, and her arches ached. She leaned harder on Lindsey and lifted her right foot slightly off the floor just to get a break from the pain.

"Watch it!" cried Lindsey. "You're breaking my arm!" It took all Lindsey's strength to push Emma back up into a straight position. "I'm letting go now, too," Lindsey told Emma. "Ready?"

Emma breathed deeply and picked up her chin. She would just ignore the pain and concentrate on keeping her balance. "Ready," she answered.

Lindsey slipped away, and for a split second Emma was poised on the toes of her shoes—then she crashed to the floor. "These things kill your feet!" she shouted as she sat on the carpet and rubbed her foot.

"That wasn't bad for a first try," said Charlie. "Let's try it again."

Emma wiggled her toes inside the shoes. She hadn't expected the shoes to hurt so much when she tried to stand on them. She'd also thought they were going to do most of the work of keeping her up. "I need to rest my feet," she told Charlie and Lindsey.

"You have to get used to the shoes," said Charlie.

"And you're not going to break them in by sitting there. Now come on."

"I guess you're right," said Emma, slowly getting up onto her feet. Once again, Lindsey and Charlie supported Emma while she wobbled on the tips of her toe shoes. The pain returned almost instantly. Emma pressed her lips together and wondered how long she could stand it. Maybe this hadn't been such a good idea after all.

"What are you girls doing?" asked Mrs. Guthrie, coming down the stairs. "Are those toe shoes, Emma?"

Startled by her mother's arrival, Emma lost what little control she had over her legs and collapsed backward onto the couch, pulling Charlie and Lindsey back with her. "Yep," she answered, brushing her hair from her eyes. "I was just trying them out."

"Where did you get the shoes?" Mrs. Guthrie asked in an astonished tone.

"We chipped in for them," Emma told her.

"You didn't have to do that," said Mrs. Guthrie, sitting on the couch and picking up Emma's foot so she could inspect the shoe. "I would have given you the money. Why didn't you ask?"

"When I asked you for the money to buy those cute imitation snakeskin boots I wanted, you said you couldn't afford them . . . so, I just figured you wouldn't have money for these, either," Emma answered.

"This is different, though," said Mrs. Guthrie, running her hand dreamily along the satin of the shoes. "These are your first toe shoes. These are special."

"You could give us the money now," suggested Emma.

"I certainly will," said her mother. "Why didn't you tell me you were going on pointe?"

"We really just decided to show that stupid Dan—" Charlie began to explain.

"I wanted to surprise you," Emma said loudly, drowning out Charlie's voice. She wasn't sure why she stopped Charlie. Maybe it was because she was enjoying her mother's attention so much. She hadn't expected her to get this excited. But now that she saw how her mother was reacting, Emma didn't want her mother's approval to turn into a lecture about simply ignoring Danielle.

"I *am* surprised, and very thrilled," her mother answered, rubbing Emma's back affectionately. "I knew that if you just stuck with it, you'd grow to love ballet. You're just like I was at your age. You have a natural ability for ballet. You have the nice long legs a dancer needs."

Charlie and Lindsey exchanged glances. It seemed to them that Mrs. Guthrie was overestimating Emma's ballet talent just a bit—but neither of them was about to tell her so. They'd never seen Mrs. Guthrie this happy about anything Emma had ever done before. They weren't about to spoil it for her, or for Emma.

"I just seem to be getting the hang of this whole ballet thing all of a sudden," Emma told her mother. She realized that what she'd said wasn't exactly true. Not really. Realistically, Emma knew she was still as terrible a dancer as ever, but having the shoes had somehow changed her attitude. The shoes made her feel so elegant—almost magical—that she suddenly *wished* she was good at ballet. And that was something she'd never felt before.

"I'm so delighted to hear you say that," said Mrs. Guthrie, beaming. "You can't imagine—" Just then the phone rang. *A client,* Emma thought, annoyed that once again her mother was being distracted by her work.

Mrs. Guthrie got up and grabbed the old black phone that sat on a wooden table. "Hello . . . yes . . . yes . . . fine, but I can't talk right now," she said, smiling at Emma. "I'm in the middle of something very important. Can I call you Monday? Very good. Talk to you then."

"What important thing are you in the middle of?" Emma asked when her mother hung up.

"Why, hearing about you going on pointe, of course," her mother answered. "This is very exciting. That client can wait."

Emma couldn't believe it. This was the first time her mother had put her before work since . . . since she had become a literary agent. Emma smiled brightly at her mother.

Mrs. Guthrie stepped back and studied her daughter. Her smile faded and was replaced by a concerned expression. "Aren't you a bit young to be on pointe?" she asked.

"Yes, in fact, I'm the only one in the beginners' class selected to go on pointe," Emma lied quickly. "Miss Claudine says I have remarkable promise. She's never seen anyone quite like me."

"That's for sure," Charlie chimed in.

Emma shot her a withering glance. "She says I'm ready to go on pointe, even though I'm just eleven," Emma continued. She was enjoying this moment too much to ruin it with the truth.

"I just knew it," said her mother. "Now aren't you sorry you made such a fuss over taking ballet? Think how far along you'd be now if you hadn't dropped out of all the other classes I enrolled you in."

"Yeah, well, who could have known?" said Emma.

"It was certainly a shock to us," added Lindsey.

"I can't wait until your first performance," Mrs. Guthrie said, her face lit with excitement.

"You won't have to wait long," said Charlie, swept up in Mrs. Guthrie's enthusiasm. "You can come see Emma a week from tomorrow. We're giving a special presentation, starring Emma on pointe."

Mrs. Guthrie's eyes opened wide with delight. "I wouldn't miss that for the world!" She leaned over and kissed Emma on the cheek. "I'm so thrilled for you, honey. Absolutely thrilled."

"Thanks, Mom," said Emma, suddenly worried. Why did Charlie have to tell her mother about the performance? She'd been enjoying her attention too much to tell the truth—but now she'd have to prove her lie.

Mrs. Guthrie rose and headed back up the stairs. "I'm ordering Chinese food, Emma," she said. "I'll get butterfly shrimp for you."

"Boy, she *is* happy!" said Emma when her mother was gone. "She usually says that butterfly shrimp is too expensive, even though it's my favorite." Emma turned and looked at Charlie. "What was the big idea of inviting my mother to class?" she hissed.

"Why not?" asked Charlie innocently. "You're going to be great. The dance I come up with is going to be terrific. Why shouldn't your mother come see you?"

"Just because, that's why," Emma grumbled.

"Don't be mad at Charlie," Lindsey said. "You're the one who lied. Why did you make up that story about being picked to go on pointe? Why didn't you just tell her the truth?"

Emma bent down and smoothed the ribbons of her shoes. "She would have told me not to do it if I told the truth," she replied. "She'd have said it was a dumb reason, and that we should just ignore Danielle."

"You usually don't care what your mother says," Charlie pointed out. "Your mother tells you not to wear makeup, and it doesn't stop you—you just put it on once you're out of the house."

"This is different," said Emma, still fiddling with her shoes. It *was* different. Her mother never got all excited just because Emma obeyed her. And she'd grown used to Emma being good at art. But this was something that had really made her stop and notice her daughter. She'd even told a client she'd call back later!

"If you say so," said Charlie with a shrug of her shoulders.

It was almost five o'clock and Charlie and Lindsey had to leave for home. Emma walked them to the

39

door. "See you tomorrow in class," said Lindsey as they were leaving.

"Yes, we'll break the good news to Miss Claudine that you're now her star pupil. I'm sure she'll be amazed to hear it," teased Charlie.

"*Shhh!*" Emma hushed her sharply, looking over her shoulder to see if her mother was nearby. "See you tomorrow."

That evening Emma and her mother sat in the eating nook of the kitchen and shared their dinner of butterfly shrimp and sautéed eggplant from Ding's restaurant. Throughout the meal, Mrs. Guthrie couldn't stop talking about ballet. "When I was your age, I wanted to be a ballerina more than anything on earth," she recalled. Emma knew this, because her mother had spoken of it often. It usually bothered Emma because it somehow placed a burden on her to be what her mother hadn't had the chance to be. And Emma wanted to be a painter, not a ballerina.

But tonight Emma wasn't annoyed. She was enjoying the warmth of her mother's approval and company.

"I have something I want to show you," said Mrs. Guthrie after dinner, as she crushed the white Chinese food cartons down into the garbage. "I'll be right back." She returned with a dusty, gray photo album and put it down on the table. "This is my album from when I was a girl."

Mrs. Guthrie sat down next to Emma and opened the book. It was full of pictures of Emma's mother and family. Many of the pictures showed Mrs. Guthrie in dance leotards, or in a tutu at a dance recital.

"I studied ballet from ten to sixteen, but I never got on pointe," her mother said sadly.

"Why not?" Emma asked.

"Oh, my family moved all the time because of your grandpa's work. My lessons were never very consistent and I never got to know any of my teachers that well. You're lucky that Miss Claudine is sensitive enough to see your potential even though you're so new to dancing. I guess all the classes you dropped out of had some effect, after all."

"Guess so," mumbled Emma, feeling guilty about her lie.

"And then I was very young when I married your father and had you. By then it was probably too late for me to have become a ballerina, anyway."

Emma didn't like the sad, faraway look in her mother's eyes. "But you like being a literary agent, don't you?" she asked.

"It's okay," her mother answered, putting her arm around Emma. "But it's not like the life you are going to have. You are going to be a ballerina!"

Chapter Four

"We have a lot of work to do today," Lindsey told Mrs. Guthrie. She and Charlie had arrived early that Sunday morning to work on their performance.

"It's so exciting," said Mrs. Guthrie. "I can't wait to see what you girls come up with. Emma's in the living room. Go right in."

Charlie and Lindsey made their way into the elegant living room and found Emma lying on the floor in front of the TV with a red crayon between her toes. "What are you *doing*?" asked Charlie. "You were supposed to be warming up so we could get right to work."

"I *am* working," said Emma, clicking off the TV with the remote control. "I've been working all morning."

"It looks to me like you're watching TV and drawing pictures with your toes," Lindsey said, picking up the sheet of white paper from under Emma's foot. It was a picture of one of the Guthries' lamps drawn in quivery lines. "This isn't bad," she commented, "considering that you did it with your foot."

"Thanks," said Emma, lying on her back and rotating her ankles in the air. "I've been drawing with my feet to strengthen my ankles. My mother told me that swirling your ankles around like this helps, too."

"Have you tried the shoes again?" asked Charlie, plopping down on the couch and turning the TV back on. She couldn't resist the wide screen in Emma's living room.

"I worked all afternoon after class yesterday," Emma replied proudly. "Seeing that conceited Danielle showing off again really got me going."

Yesterday's class had been very exciting to Emma. Suddenly the exercises at the barre had taken on a new meaning. She saw them as ways to strengthen and limber her legs so that she'd be able to get up on her toes. She concentrated as she never had before. Miss Claudine noticed the change immediately. "Very good work today, mademoiselle," she said. "Your best ever."

Danielle had once again demonstrated her pointe work. This time Emma was less ready to make fun when Danielle stumbled or her leg shook. She now knew how difficult it was to do even the simplest looking step.

That didn't make her like Danielle any better, though. And Emma decided that if a twit like Danielle could master the shoes, then she could, too.

"Can you believe her parents showed up *again* just to watch her? I would be too embarrassed if they were my parents," said Lindsey.

"Yeah," mumbled Emma, climbing to her feet. She didn't like talking about Danielle's parents. She hated the fact that she envied the attention they paid to Danielle. Emma felt she was much too cool to be jealous of a twerp like Danielle. Yet, again and again, her mind would wander and she'd picture herself in her new toe shoes, her mother and father standing at the door of Miss Claudine's studio yelling "Brava!"—just as Danielle's parents had. She didn't want to have this daydream, but it just kept drifting back into her head when she wasn't paying attention.

"Let's go down to your basement and get to it," said Lindsey, pulling off her denim jacket.

"I have some great ideas," added Charlie. "I was watching this movie-of-the-week thing about an English girl who wants to become a great dancer, and just when she's about to make her debut, the Nazis bomb the theater and a brick falls on her head and she develops a split personality, but then her boyfriend— she thinks he's a soldier, but he's really a duke—he looks for her, and—"

"Charlie," sighed Lindsey, "get to the point! What's your idea?"

"Okay, I'm getting to it," said Charlie. "In the end, she does this great dance on pointe. I paid close attention and I think I remember a lot of the steps. So, we can use them. Plus I have my ballet book from the library."

"Well, let's go then," said Lindsey, bending to pick up the purple toe shoes that were on the floor by the couch.

"Wait, let me pick them up." Emma stood. She stuck out her foot and grabbed the backs of the shoes between her toes and lifted them. "I haven't bent over once in three days," she explained seriously. "I'm picking everything up with my feet to strengthen my toes."

The girls went down to Emma's basement and put on their leotards. Emma popped a tape called *Favorite Ballet Pieces* into the stereo. Her mother had bought it the other day especially for Emma.

Charlie opened her book and took out the stick figure diagrams she'd drawn while watching the TV movie. Emma put on a pair of thin white socks instead of wearing her tights. She hoped the thinner material would make the shoes pinch less. She laced them up as Lindsey fast-forwarded the tape, looking for some music she liked.

Yesterday afternoon after class, Emma had discovered that she could get onto her toes by leaning on the card table. At first she'd had to put both hands on the table. Now, after much practice, she was able to keep only one hand down most of the time, occasionally steadying herself with two hands.

The problem was that, even with the support of the table, her feet hurt terribly. Emma's second toes were longer than the others, so her entire weight was concentrated there. The joints of those toes bent and pressed against the shoes, rubbing every time she moved. Besides that, the small toe of her right foot was squeezed uncomfortably against the toe next to it. It didn't take long for all ten toes and her arches to start throbbing unbearably.

"Okay," said Charlie. "To start, I think you should hold your arms in front of you in a circle and sort of take tiny steps across the floor."

Emma pushed herself up onto her toes. She had to slap her hands down on the card table twice before she was able to balance. Then, waving her arms wildly on either side to help her stay up, she set out, heading for the couch. She'd only taken one step before she fell to the ground.

"It's no use," she moaned.

"I know," said Lindsey. "Let's put the furniture close together, and you can practice going from one piece to the other. Then we'll gradually move the furniture farther and farther apart."

"Brilliant," agreed Charlie, pushing a large, cushioned chair next to the card table. Lindsey and Charlie quickly pulled all the furniture into a lopsided circle in the middle of the room.

Emma climbed to her feet and spent the next fifteen minutes on her toes, supporting herself with one piece of furniture and then tottering over to the next piece. Finally she fell down into the chair. "I can't do this anymore," she complained. "My feet hurt too much."

"Stop complaining and—*eeeewww!* Look at your feet!" said Charlie, pointing at the foot Emma had dangled over the side of the chair.

Emma winced when she saw the smear of blood on her right ankle just above the shoe. Gingerly, she untied the ribbons and took off her shoe. Peeling back her sock, she saw a large broken blister on the inside of her heel. "See, I told you they hurt," she said in a pained voice. She undid the other shoe and saw a smaller blister forming on her left heel.

Lindsey knelt and examined Emma's feet. "You have bony feet," she commented.

"I do not," Emma said, drawing her feet up under herself. "I have normal feet. There must be something wrong with the shoes."

"There's nothing wrong with these shoes," Charlie said, trying to wipe away the small bloodstain on the shoe with her thumb. "In the movie I saw, they showed the girl learning to go on pointe. She was crying and rubbing her feet all the time. Just when she was about to quit, her old Russian ballet teacher told her, 'To be great, you must suffer.' "

"And what did the girl say?" asked Emma.

"I don't know, because they had a commercial. But when the commercial was over, the girl was dancing great—so I guess she suffered in the scenes we didn't see. You know how TV is."

"I wish *this* was TV, then," grumbled Emma, rubbing her feet. "I could miss out on the suffering part."

"That's not the point," said Charlie. "The point is that even if it hurts a little, you have to keep working. My brothers are always saying, 'no pain, no gain.' "

"Your brothers play football," Lindsey pointed out. "It's not the same. I don't think blisters are so great for you."

"Well," said Charlie, "when my brother John was on the gymnastics team in school, he did the parallel bars and his hands got all ripped up with blisters. I saw him soaking them in a bowl of vinegar one day. He said that made them tougher so the blisters didn't hurt as much."

"I never heard of that," Lindsey said skeptically.

"All I know is what he told me."

"I might as well try it," said Emma. "I've got to

do something." The girls went upstairs and found some vinegar in Emma's kitchen. They poured it into a bowl and brought it back down to the basement.

"Here goes," said Emma as she sat on the big chair and lifted her heel over the bowl on the floor. Carefully, she dunked her heel in. *"Aaaaaahhh!"* she screamed, pulling her foot up quickly. "Are you crazy, Charlie? That burns like anything!"

Charlie stared into the bowl as if looking for a shark or some other hazard she hadn't anticipated. "It's just vinegar," she said, swooshing her finger around in the smelly liquid.

"Well, vinegar and blisters don't mix," grumbled Emma.

"Remember, you have to suffer if you wish to be great," said Charlie.

"Oh, don't give me your TV words of wisdom!" Emma snapped. "My feet are a mess and this vinegar isn't going to help them."

"I guess there's no sense trying to do any more today," said Lindsey, pulling her jeans on over her leotard. "Do you think we should give this whole idea up?"

Lindsey and Charlie stood, waiting for Emma's answer. Emma pressed her lips together thoughtfully. "Maybe," she said. "I don't know . . . maybe."

"See how your blisters feel tomorrow," suggested Lindsey.

Lindsey and Charlie finished dressing and said good-bye to Emma. They had only been gone a few minutes when the basement phone rang. Emma lay back on the couch, listening to it ring. Her mother usually picked it up in two rings, but the phone just kept ringing.

Emma sighed, annoyed at being roused from her dreary state on the couch. *Mom's probably in the shower,* she thought as she hobbled over to the phone. "Hello," she answered sharply.

"Hello, yourself," came a familiar voice on the other end. "Do you always answer the phone so cheerfully?"

"Daddy!" Emma cried, brightening immediately. "I didn't know it was going to be you. I thought it would be one of Mom's stupid clients. They're always calling here every second."

"Yes, I imagine that could get annoying," he said. He sounded more amused than sincere to Emma. "Anyway, I called to tell you that I will be able to come and see your performance, after all."

"My perfor—what?" Emma stuttered.

"Your mother was so excited when she called me the other night. She said Miss Claudine picked you out of all the others to go on pointe. That's wonderful, sweetheart."

"Yeah, well it's not as big a deal as it sounds."

"It's a very big deal," he said proudly. "She told me that you'll be giving a special performance in front of the class. I was going to go away for the weekend on business but I canceled it. I wouldn't miss this for anything."

"You broke a business appointment just to come see me?" Emma asked happily.

"I certainly did," her father said.

"That's really nice of you," Emma told him, basking in the warmth of his attention. "You and Mom are coming together? Dawn isn't coming, is she?" Emma had met his girlfriend Dawn, and she didn't like her. She resented her father having a girlfriend— a young and pretty one—whom he seemed to value more than he did Emma. It made Emma happy that he had chosen her over business *and* Dawn.

"No," her father assured her, laughing nervously. "Dawn had other plans." He sounded uncomfortable, as he always did whenever the subject of Dawn came up.

Emma heaved a sigh of relief. "That's too bad," she said politely, not wanting to spoil the nice moment with her usual anti-Dawn remarks.

"My other phone is ringing—I have to go," her father said hurriedly. "Tell your mother I called. Love you, pumpkin."

"I love—" Emma began, but her father had already hung up. It seemed he was always in a hurry— picking up the other ringing phone, going into a meeting, running late for an appointment. She tried to accept the fact that that was just his way, but sometimes it made her angry. Really angry. She was supposed to see him on the weekends and half the time he couldn't even make it.

Emma picked the purple toe shoes off the floor and ran her fingers along their smooth surface. Her father was coming especially to see her dance. He'd even canceled a business meeting!

Her daydream was coming true. Her parents would be standing in the doorway of Miss Claudine's—just as Danielle's parents had—and they would be watch-

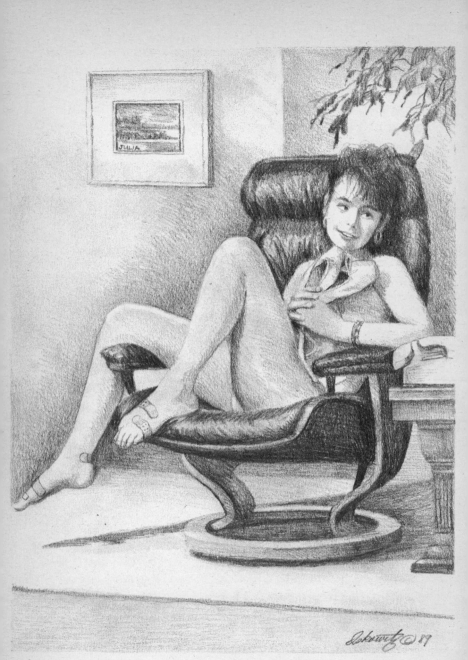

ing proudly as Emma danced on her toes, the center of attention. Her mother wouldn't be thinking of her clients, and her father would put aside thoughts of his law practice and his girlfriend, at least for the afternoon. For once, their attention would be focused completely on Emma.

Emma shut her eyes and pictured her parents clapping proudly. She saw her father holding a large bouquet of roses, and her mother's eyes filled with tears of happiness.

It was a wonderful fantasy, but there was just one problem. One huge problem. Emma couldn't dance on pointe. In fact, the way her feet felt, she didn't know if she could dance at all.

Now what do I do? Emma asked herself. She could just admit defeat. Who would really care? Her mother and father, that's who. They'd say they understood, but Emma didn't want to let them down. It felt too good to have them praising her and paying attention to her. The thought of going back to being plain old Emma, lost in the shuffle of their busy lives, was too depressing.

No, there was no choice. She simply had to master the toe shoes. Emma crossed the room and sat in the big chair. She stared down at the bowl of vinegar at her feet. "No pain, no gain," she muttered as she winced and dipped her heel in once again. The blister burned and tears came to her eyes. She dug her nails into the arms of the chair. *I'd better be a great dancer when this is over,* she thought, *because I sure am suffering.*

Chapter Five

"Okay, now, we'll spin toward you from either side of the room," Charlie instructed. It was the Friday afternoon before their performance, and Charlie, Emma, and Lindsey were at the Munsons', still figuring out the steps they would do. Most of the ideas Charlie had taken from the TV movie had to be scrapped because they were just too difficult. They had simplified their routine, but it was still an odd mixture of steps they'd learned in class and new ones they'd tried to teach themselves from reading Charlie's library book.

"What am I supposed to do while you guys are spinning around the place?" asked Emma with a scowl on her face. In the last week, Emma had worked very hard to master the toe shoes. She'd continued rotating her ankles. She did it two hundred times every night before bed. She also dunked her feet into the vinegar every night. This experience grew more painful as the number and size of the blisters on Emma's feet continued to grow. As far as Emma could see, the vinegar wasn't doing anything except stinging and giving her feet a peculiar smell. Still, she had to try everything that might help her.

"You've been so crabby lately," Charlie told Emma.

"You'd be crabby, too, if your feet were killing you," Emma snapped back. Emma's feet hurt all the time now. Last Wednesday's ballet class had been such a painful experience that Emma had pretended to be sick in order to be allowed to sit down.

"Aren't you using the vinegar?" Charlie asked.

"That vinegar is a dumb idea," retorted Emma. "And how am I supposed to dance when I can barely walk?"

"If you want to wimp out now, that's your business," Charlie said, folding her arms across her chest sternly.

"I didn't say I was going to do that," growled Emma. "I just said my feet hurt, okay?"

"We don't have to do this at all, you know," Lindsey broke into the agrument. "I feel kind of dumb about the whole thing, to tell you the truth. We've lied to your mother. Plus, Miss Claudine told us not to do any steps she hasn't taught us. And we don't even know the dance yet. I think we should just forget it."

"We *have* to do it," Emma insisted. "Miss Claudine has set the time aside for us already."

Lindsey sighed. "Well if you're sure you want to do this, then let's get to work—so we don't make total jerks of ourselves," she said. "Emma, you're supposed to be up on your toes just kind of tippy-toeing around while we spin around you."

"That's going to look stupid," Emma grouched.

"Emma, since you can't do anything else besides hop up on your toes for a few seconds at a time, we don't exactly have too many choices, do we?" said Charlie.

"Okay, okay," Emma agreed. After a week of trying, Emma *was* able to get up and move a few steps forward and backward before clomping back down onto her heels. Charlie had suggested, quite sensibly, that they should construct their dance around that rather than have Emma try to do anything more difficult. The result was a dance that featured Charlie and Lindsey twirling and leaping in front of and behind Emma, while Emma stood in the middle and kept trying to stay on her toes for as long as possible.

By five o'clock Emma was once again on the verge of tears. Her feet were sore and achy. "I can't do any more," she told her friends in a weak voice.

"I think we're in pretty good shape," said Charlie, trying to be encouraging. "It looks pretty good."

"The important thing is that Emma is up on her toes," added Lindsey. "That's really what we wanted to prove—that anybody could do it."

"Thanks a lot!" said Emma.

"You know what I mean—that Danielle isn't the only one who can dance on pointe."

Emma nodded and threw herself down on the couch. Charlie and Lindsey could say what they liked, but she knew the dance was terrible, a total embarrassment. And Emma had always prided herself on being very cool. She wasn't one to go out and make a fool of herself.

"You rest a minute while we go over our part," said Lindsey.

"That's a good idea," Emma agreed. She stretched out on the couch and pretended to be busy chipping the purple polish from her nails. She tried to appear calm, but inside she was panicking. She wished she could just disappear. Then it occurred to her. She could run away. She wouldn't have to perform the next day—and she wouldn't have to explain why. Not to anyone. But where would she go? She had lots of friends in Manhattan, but their parents would all call her mother. If she was going to run away, she had to have some place to run to. And she didn't.

"I'm going home," said Charlie after a while.

"I'll walk with you," Emma told her as she slipped the toe shoes from her tender feet and put her clothes on over her leotard.

Lindsey walked them upstairs and to the front door. "Don't worry, Emma," she said. "It really looks okay."

"Sure," Emma said, smiling faintly.

She followed Charlie across Lindsey's front lawn. "Can't you walk any faster?" Charlie asked. "I have to be home for supper. It's my day to set the table."

"This is as fast as I can walk," Emma answered as she limped along behind Charlie. "Honest." Just then Emma stopped. "Darn! I left my bag at Lindsey's. I have to go back and get it."

"Do you mind if I don't wait?" Charlie asked. "I really have to get going."

"Sure, go ahead." Emma headed back to Lindsey's house. When she got to the front step, she saw that

57

Lindsey had forgotten to shut the inside door. She tried the storm door. It was open, too.

She knocked on the glass, but there was no answer. She was about to ring the doorbell when she suddenly had a daring idea. She could run away to Lindsey's basement!

It sounded crazy, but it might work. Lindsey's father kept a big refrigerator down there and it was stocked with food that didn't fit into the upstairs fridge. The basement wasn't very warm or cozy, so Lindsey and her father didn't go down there much—just to do laundry and get stuff from the refrigerator. She could hide in the paneled-off boiler room if she heard someone coming.

With her heart thumping, Emma slowly opened the door and crept back into the front hallway. She'd been in Lindsey's home lots of times, but now she suddenly felt like a prowler. *I'm not hurting Lindsey,* she reminded herself. *I'm just borrowing her basement for a little while.*

Slowly, Emma crept across Lindsey's living room, into the hall, and down the basement stairs. The basement had a boiler room, a laundry room, and a back room where Mr. Munson kept his tools and the refrigerator. The middle of the basement was cluttered with some old furniture, bikes, trunks, and boxes. The sun was setting and the basement was quite dark, but Emma didn't dare turn on a light for fear of attracting attention. She saw an old quilt thrown in the corner that she laid out behind a high stack of boxes. *This isn't so bad,* she told herself as she settled down on it.

It didn't take more than ten minutes for Emma to feel uncomfortable sitting there all alone in the dark. She was amazed at how much she could hear in the quiet house. She heard the shower water from the upstairs bathroom and the sound of the toilet flushing. She jumped when the boiler kicked in with a loud bang. She heard the sound of Mr. Munson's car as he pulled into the driveway, and she could even hear the clattering of his keys as he threw them on the kitchen counter.

Emma felt strange, as if she were a ghost haunting someone's house. Although she wasn't due home for supper for several hours, she was suddenly starving. Yet she didn't dare cross the basement to reach the refrigerator—which now seemed a hundred miles away—for fear of making noise.

After a while, she heard Lindsey and her father talking in the kitchen, and the smell of supper cooking made her hungrier still. She squirmed uncomfortably on her quilt.

I need a plan, she told herself. *Tomorrow is the performance. If I stay away just a few days after that, then everyone will be so glad to see me that they'll forget all about my dancing on pointe.*

Emma tried to picture what would happen. Her parents would be frantic. They might even call the police! If they did that, she might get into big trouble when she finally showed up. Maybe they'd say they couldn't control her and throw her in a home for delinquents. *Ha!* thought Emma bitterly. *Sure. Then they'd never have to pay any attention to me ever again.*

A feeling of panic swept over Emma. What had she

gotten herself into? She should go home right now. But she couldn't—not with Lindsey and her father eating in the kitchen. They'd probably watch TV in the living room after that. She couldn't just emerge from their basement and say, "Hi, folks, I took a wrong turn on my way home and ended up in your basement." She could wait until they went to bed, but by then she'd already be in big trouble. And the thought of walking all the way home in the dark frightened her.

It was all too much! She was in this stupid jam just because she'd wanted a little attention from her parents. How had it all gone so wrong? Overwhelmed, Emma laid down and pulled a corner of the quilt over her head. She squeezed her eyes shut tight and wished she'd never seen a pair of toe shoes in her life.

Chapter Six

Emma drifted in and out of sleep. She had a series of brief dreams. In one dream, she was a ghost, floating unseen over her parents' heads. They were in their old apartment in the city and they were searching for something. They turned over all the cushions and rummaged through the closets. "Where is Emma?" Mrs. Guthrie asked. "She must be here somewhere."

"I haven't seen her since she was a baby," Mr. Guthrie answered. "How could we have been so careless? How could we have misplaced our little girl?"

"I'm up here, Daddy!" Emma cried in her dream. "Mommy, it's me, Emma! Come get me." But they couldn't hear her. They kept on looking—under the couch, behind the chairs. "I'm here!" Emma screamed to them. "I'm right here!"

"Okay, Emma, okay! Wake up!" Emma looked up and saw Lindsey staring down at her. Startled, she rolled into a crouch. Then she remembered where she was.

She grinned sheepishly, trying to cover her embarrassment. "Hi," she said.

"Hi!" Lindsey yelped. "What the heck are you doing here? Are you crazy?"

"I didn't think you'd find me," Emma said.

"I wouldn't have, except that when I came down to get my shirt from the dryer I heard you yelling 'I'm here! I'm here!' That's not exactly a smart thing to do when you're trying to hide."

"I guess I was dreaming."

"You still haven't answered my question," Lindsey insisted, kneeling down beside Emma. "What *are* you doing sleeping down in my basement? If you wanted to sleep over, you should have just asked. What's going on?"

Emma couldn't keep it in any longer. She told Lindsey the whole story. " . . . and now my father is driving all the way in to see me dance tomorrow. Except that I can't dance. You know that I'm terrible. Admit it, I am."

"Well . . . yes . . . you are," Lindsey agreed. "But it's not really your fault. It was dumb to think we could get you on pointe without Miss Claudine's help. I read in Charlie's ballet book that you're supposed to have studied ballet for *at least* two years before going on pointe. I think we should just forget the whole thing."

"I can't," said Emma, burying her face in her hands. "My parents are so excited to see me dance. I can't let them down."

"They'll understand if you tell them you tried, but that you just couldn't do it," said Lindsey kindly.

Emma got a dreamy, faraway look in her eye. "There's another part to this, too. This will be the

first time my mother and father have done anything together since they got divorced. They'll probably take me out to eat after the class. It will be just like it used to be."

"It must be rough, having your parents be divorced," Lindsey sympathized.

"It stinks," Emma said. "You try to tell yourself it's for the best. And maybe it is. But it still stinks."

"Boy, I thought all you cared about was making Danielle mad," said Lindsey. "And the whole time you were hardly thinking about her at all. You were thinking about your parents."

Emma shook her head sadly. "I wanted them to notice me. That's all."

"You know what? Your mother has probably noticed you're gone already," Lindsey pointed out. "It's past seven. Were you planning on staying here all night?"

"Sort of," Emma answered, feeling completely foolish. "I guess I figured I'd just sort of hide out from the whole thing."

"That was kind of dumb."

"I know," Emma replied. "I didn't know what else to—" Emma stopped short when she heard Mr. Munson's footsteps on the basement stairs.

"Lindsey," he called. "Emma's mother just called. Do you have any idea where she could be?"

Emma and Lindsey looked at one another. Now what? Emma was usually the quick thinker of the group, but in her panic her mind was blank.

"Ummm . . . yeah, Dad," Lindsey called back. "She's . . . um . . . she's . . . here."

"What!" The overhead light snapped on and Mr. Munson hurried down the stairs.

"What did you do that for?" Emma hissed in a low whisper.

"What else was I supposed to say?" Lindsey whispered back.

The two girls stood up and faced Lindsey's father. "Care to tell me what's going on?" he asked.

Lindsey shifted her weight nervously from one foot to the other. "I meant to ask you if Emma could sleep over and she meant to ask her mother. But we both forgot and Emma just went ahead and fell asleep, and then I forgot that she was down here sleeping. So I couldn't remember to ask you if she could sleep over since I forgot she was sleeping over in the first place. And then—"

"Never mind!" cried Mr. Munson. "Just come upstairs and call your mother right now, Emma. She's frantic worrying about you." Mr. Munson hurried back up the steps. "Look, Emma, as long as you're here, why don't you sleep over for real."

"Thanks," said Emma.

"Once you tell your mother where you are, maybe you should tell her the truth about dancing on pointe," Lindsey suggested.

"I think you're right," Emma agreed. "I will."

Calling from the kitchen phone, Emma took Lindsey's advice and told her mother the same story about the sleeping over "mix-up." After Mrs. Guthrie calmed down, she accepted her daughter's excuse.

Emma wiped her hand down her face miserably. "Mom, listen, there's something I want to tell you."

Emma looked at Lindsey, and then turned her back to her. "I . . . I . . . uh, umm . . . I . . ."

Emma was quiet and Lindsey could vaguely hear the hum of Mrs. Guthrie's voice as she chattered on excitedly over the phone.

"Yes, Mom. I'm excited, too, Mom. I know, I know. It's great," Emma answered her mother in a flat tone. "Mom, please listen to me a minute. What I have to tell you is that . . . that . . . I just want to say that . . . I'm real happy you and Dad are coming tomorrow. That's all. Okay, bye." Emma spoke the words very quickly and then hung up the phone with a bang. "Don't look at me like that," she said with her back still to Lindsey.

"You can't even see me. How do you know I'm even looking at you?" Lindsey cried, growing frustrated with Emma's strange behavior.

"Because I know you. I just couldn't tell her, all right?" Emma said, turning to face her friend. "She kept going on and on about how excited she was and how proud of me and all. Oh, Lindsey, what am I going to do?"

"Well," said Lindsey, leaning back against the kitchen counter. "I can only think of one thing." She punched Charlie's number into the phone. "Hi," she said when Charlie picked up. "You have to ask your parents if you can stay over at my house tonight." Charlie argued that it was late, but Lindsey assured her it was important.

An hour later, Charlie appeared at Lindsey's front door. She waved good-bye to her mother in the car outside and came in wearing a frown. "I think you should warn a person when you suddenly have an urge for a slumber party in the middle of the night," she grumbled, throwing her overnight bag down in the front hall.

"This is an emergency," Lindsey told her seriously. "Emma has to look good tomorrow. We have at least twelve more hours to practice before our show tomorrow."

"Are you kidding?" cried Charlie. "I have to sleep."

"She's right," Emma agreed.

"Don't you remember?" cried Lindsey, doing her best imitation of a Russian accent. "If you vant to be great, you haff to suffer!"

Chapter Seven

At nine-thirty the next morning, Emma, Charlie, and Lindsey sat at Lindsey's kitchen table with their eyes half open and their heads propped up sleepily on their hands. "I was so wide awake at four in the morning," mumbled Lindsey. "I don't understand why I'm so tired now."

Emma was dreamily munching her cereal. "I know what you mean," she said, yawning. She lifted up her head and looked around. "What's that sound?"

Lindsey reached across the table and pulled away the cereal box Charlie had been reading as she ate. Behind it was Charlie, her head nestled on her arm, snoring loudly. "Wake up," Emma said, reaching over and jostling Charlie's arm.

"What? Huh?" Charlie sputtered, rousing from her sleep and looking up at her friends with sleepy eyes. "Oh! Hi, guys." She rubbed her eyes. "Let's go back to sleep for a little while."

"Can't," Lindsey told her as she began clearing the dishes. "We have to take showers and be ready to leave by ten-thirty."

Charlie grunted and slid down in her chair until only her eyes and the top of her head showed above the table. "The next time you feel like inviting me over to practice ballet steps all night, try to forget my phone number, okay?"

"I think it was worth it," Lindsey insisted. "The whole dance looks much better now."

"Do you really think so?" asked Emma hopefully. "You're not just saying that?"

"No," said Lindsey. "It's really much, much better."

The girls showered and dressed for class. By ten-thirty, Charlie and Lindsey were standing outside in the driveway with Mr. Munson, waiting for Emma. "It takes her forever to put that stupid makeup on," grumbled Lindsey.

"She told me she's not wearing any today," said Charlie, "because her parents will be there. You know her mother doesn't really like her to wear makeup at all. Most of the stuff she sneaks."

"What's keeping her, then?" Lindsey wondered as she climbed into the front seat of the car.

"At last," said Mr. Munson when Emma finally emerged from the front door. He got behind the wheel of the car and turned on the engine. "Let's get a move on," he called to her.

Emma looked up and smiled weakly. She tried to hurry toward the car, but the blisters on her feet made her limp. At four o'clock last night they hadn't felt too bad. Now they were worse than ever. Much worse. Practicing all night hadn't been such a great idea as far as her feet were concerned. Sure, Charlie and Lindsey knew their parts better—and so did Emma. But now her feet were not only blistered, but swollen as well.

"You just have to get through today," Charlie whispered as Emma climbed into the backseat beside her.

Emma nodded bravely. "Just a few more hours, really."

The trip to the mall went too quickly for Emma. Before she knew it, she was hobbling down the lower ramp to Miss Claudine's. As they entered they saw Miss Claudine in the front room. *"Bonjour, chéries,"* she greeted them cheerily. "Your mother just called me, Mademoiselle Emma. She wanted to confirm the time of your performance in class today. She seemed quite excited."

"Yes, she is," Emma told her in a small, flat voice.

Miss Claudine narrowed her eyes and leaned forward to look at Emma more closely. "Do you feel all right, *chérie?*"

Emma nodded and her nostrils flared slightly as she suppressed a yawn. "Just tired, that's all."

"We had a ballet slumber party last night," said Charlie.

"I see," said Miss Claudine, smoothing the top of her ash-blond hair. "Hurry and change so we can begin class."

The girls changed in the narrow dressing room, along with the rest of the beginners' class. Danielle was there, already dressed in her black leotard. Charlie and Lindsey shot smug smiles her way. "What are you two smirking about?" Danielle snapped at them irritably.

"You'll find out," said Lindsey coolly as she pulled on her baby-blue tights.

"Yes, you'll see," added Charlie.

Danielle's eyes darted to Emma suspiciously, knowing that she was usually at the center of any mischief. But Emma was too busy carefully peeling back her socks so she wouldn't rip off any of the many bandages that now covered her feet. She paid no attention to Danielle.

As Emma put her arm into her leotard sleeve she sensed someone's eyes on her. She looked up and saw that Miss Claudine had come into the dressing room to talk to Danielle about helping her order new leotards for the next session. As usual, Danielle stood pertly at attention, gazing adoringly at Miss Claudine as she spoke. "I'd love to help you, Miss Claudine," Danielle crooned. "It's no trouble at all."

But Emma realized that Miss Claudine was only giving Danielle part of her attention. While she listened to her, her eyes looked over Danielle's shoulder, focusing on Emma.

Emma met Miss Claudine's gaze and smiled, but her teacher didn't smile back. Miss Claudine's serious expression made Emma uncomfortable, so she ducked her head down and busied herself with her soft flat ballet shoes. How nice and comfortable they felt compared with the stiff toe shoes hidden in Emma's pocketbook.

The dressing room was emptying out. "Come on," said Lindsey from the doorway.

"Go ahead, I'll be right there," Emma told her.

"Okay," Lindsey said, hurrying off to class.

In another minute Danielle left. Miss Claudine stood where she was and studied Emma for another moment. "Mademoiselle Emma, something *is* wrong," she said finally. "I've been watching you, and I can see that you've hurt yourself."

Emma didn't know what to say. "It's . . . I . . . not really," she stammered. Yet there was something in Miss Claudine's voice that touched Emma. Her teacher's concern made Emma want to pour her heart out, but she was afraid to speak.

"It's your feet, isn't it?" Miss Claudine continued. "You've injured them somehow."

"Just a little blister."

"Sit," said Miss Claudine, directing Emma over to the long bench in the dressing room. Miss Claudine knelt and slipped Emma's ballet shoe from her right foot. "What are all these bandages for?" she asked in a shocked voice when she saw the outlines of the many bandages that showed through Emma's tights. "And this one is bleeding still!" she added, pointing to a spot of blood that had come through the heel of Emma's tights.

Miss Claudine looked up at Emma, her sharp blue eyes full of questions and concern. Emma suddenly felt very silly, but she knew the time had come to admit the truth. "I've been trying to teach myself to dance on pointe."

"Oh, Emma, *chérie!*" cried Miss Claudine. "That was very foolish. *Very* foolish. You could have hurt yourself—not only your feet, but your legs, and even

73

your hips. This isn't something a person can teach herself. I require that my students study ballet for at least two years before going on pointe. Besides that, I would never put an eleven-year-old on pointe. It could hurt the development of your ankles."

"But Danielle—"

"Danielle is almost thirteen and has been studying ballet since she was three! She practices every day, and has for years. What made you decide to do this?"

Emma didn't want to meet Miss Claudine's eyes. She folded her hands in her lap and studied her nails. "I got so sick of Danielle showing off all the time. I wanted to show that she wasn't the only one who could dance on pointe."

Miss Claudine sat back on her heels and looked at Emma. "Was that the only reason?" she asked gently.

Tears welled up in Emma's eyes. "Not really . . ." She told Miss Claudine all about her parents and how she couldn't let them down.

"Your mother and father will understand," said Miss Claudine, brushing some stray hairs from Emma's forehead. "I can't let you give this performance today. You realize that, of course."

Emma stiffened with panic. "You have to. Please. My father is coming all the way in from the city. He canceled all his plans for this weekend just to see me. Please! Please!"

"I'm sorry, Emma, but I can't. You can barely walk."

"But, Miss Claudine, I won't be able to face my parents."

"I'm sorry, but it is impossible—"

74

Just then there was a sharp rap outside the dressing room door. "It's me, Claudine. Can I come in?" asked a familiar male voice.

"Yes, come in," Miss Claudine called.

Adrian stood in the doorway looking as handsome as ever in faded blue jeans and a jean jacket worn over a red sweater. "Hi," he said with a smile. "I was heading downtown to class, and I thought I'd stop by and see if you wanted to take in a movie tonight."

"Yes, that sounds nice," Miss Claudine answered absently. She looked quickly at Emma and then back to Adrian. "You've got your dance things with you, right?" she asked him.

Adrian nodded. "In the car."

"You don't have to be at your class until two. Can I ask you for a small favor?"

"Sure," he said, leaning against the doorframe, his eyes alive with curiosity.

Miss Claudine rose to her feet. "Mademoiselle Emma has a problem and I think you may be just the person to help us solve it."

Emma looked at her teacher hopefully. What was Miss Claudine thinking?

Miss Claudine narrowed her eyes and tapped the tips of her graceful fingers together thoughtfully. "Yes, I think this will work," she said quietly. "This will do the trick."

Chapter Eight

Miss Claudine insisted that Emma not take class. She brought a folding chair into the studio and told her to sit and just observe the class. "But what about the performance?" Emma asked.

"You will have your performance, *chérie,*" Miss Claudine told her. "Adrian is going to help you. He's thinking about the best way to do it right now. He'll explain it all to you when he's ready."

Miss Claudine then went to the center of the studio and took over from Danielle, who had been leading the class through their warm-up exercises. Charlie and Lindsey cast worried glances over at Emma. They were dying to know what was going on, but there was no chance to speak to her.

"Do you think we're going to have our performance?" Lindsey whispered to Charlie as they pliéd side by side at the barre.

"Doesn't look like it," Charlie whispered back. "I wonder why Miss Claudine is making Emma sit."

"I can guess," said Lindsey.

After a while, Charlie and Lindsey noticed that

Adrian had come into the studio. He crouched down next to Emma and began talking to her in a low whisper. He was using his hands in hurried gestures. "He looks like he's explaining a football play to her," Lindsey observed.

"I wish I knew what was going on," said Charlie, so busy watching Emma that she tottered forward out of her arabesque position.

It was nearly twelve-thirty when Mrs. Guthrie stuck her head into the studio. When she saw Emma sitting, she mouthed the words, "Are you okay?"

Emma nodded and mouthed, "Where's Dad?" back at her mother. Mrs. Guthrie pointed over her shoulder. As she did, Emma's tall, handsome father appeared in the doorway. He flashed his dazzling smile at Emma and stepped into the room.

Miss Claudine took the needle off the record she was playing during the class. "Today we have a special event, class," she announced. "Some of your classmates have put together a dance routine on their own, and they are going to perform it for us today. It features Mesdemoiselles Lindsey, Charlotte, and Emma."

"I don't believe this," sighed Danielle loud enough for all to hear. "*Those* three?"

Charlie and Lindsey glared at Danielle, then got up and walked to the center of the room. Emma had gone to the dressing room to put on the purple toe shoes while Miss Claudine had been talking. Trying not to limp too much, she joined the others.

"Today's performance also features a special guest dancer, your friend and mine, Monsieur Adrian."

Miss Claudine gestured toward the studio door as Adrian made his way past the Guthries. He was dressed in a black sweat suit and gray sneakers.

"Boy, you can tell he's a dancer even in a sweat suit," Charlie whispered. "Look how straight he stands." Adrian spread his arms wide while the class applauded him.

"Ham," Miss Claudine joked in a loud whisper.

"What's he doing here?" Lindsey asked Emma, speaking under her breath.

"Just do what we planned," Emma told them. "Adrian's going to help me out."

Charlie and Lindsey looked at Emma and shrugged their shoulders. "Whatever you say," said Charlie skeptically.

Miss Claudine put in the cassette and found the music Emma had told her to play. Charlie and Lindsey took their positions diagonally opposite each other, with Emma standing in the center.

"Miss Claudine!" Danielle interrupted the proceedings. "Why is she wearing toe shoes?"

"We will talk about the dance later," Miss Claudine put her off. Charlie and Lindsey looked at one another and giggled. Danielle was clearly irritated to see Emma on pointe.

Miss Claudine pressed the "play" button and the music began. At the same time, Charlie and Lindsey began twirling toward Emma. As they'd rehearsed, Emma raised her arms in front of her and scooted up onto her toes.

But before she could fall forward or back, Adrian

swooped in and lifted Emma off her feet, holding her high over his head.

Adrian had told Emma he would do this, but nothing could have prepared her for the thrill of being carried in his arms like a real ballerina! He was so strong and confident that Emma wasn't even concerned about falling. She extended her arms out as gracefully as she could, while Adrian walked in a small circle, holding her.

He set her gently down onto the floor. Charlie and Lindsey faced one another on either side of Emma and did arabesques. Again Adrian stepped in, and this time he lifted Emma straight up in front of him. Getting into the swing of things, Emma fluttered her feet back and forth as she went up. For a second she felt as though she were lighter than air and could actually float off the ground.

When Adrian once again set Emma onto the ground, Charlie and Lindsey began doing their little jumps in a circle around Emma. All their movements had been planned to disguise the fact that Emma wasn't really doing much, but now they didn't have to hide anything. Emma looked regal and convincing as Adrian picked her up around the waist and dipped forward slightly with Emma held tightly in the crook of his arm.

The music swelled and came to its final exciting climax. Charlie and Lindsey twirled and fell to their knees, extending their arms up dramatically in Emma's direction. For one last time, Emma scooted up onto her toes and was lifted into the air by Adrian.

For a moment there was silence. Then Emma

heard the sound of one person applauding. It was her father—she could tell by the loudness of the clapping. Right behind that was the fast clattering clap of her mother. As she hovered there in the air, Emma felt like a dream was coming true.

Soon the whole class was applauding. Adrian put Emma down. He held her hand as they stood with Charlie and Lindsey and bowed for the class. Emma turned to her parents and smiled at them. "Brava!" called Mr. Guthrie, wearing a smile. "Brava!"

"*Très bien!* Very good!" Miss Claudine said. She turned to the class. "We'll talk about this dance on Wednesday, but time has run out for now. *Au revoir, chéries.*" Miss Claudine then went over to Adrian and kissed him lightly on the lips. "*Merci beaucoup,* my love," she said.

His eyes twinkled merrily. "It was a breeze with such a graceful ballerina for a partner."

Emma grinned at him. "Thanks," she said.

"Any time," he replied. "I've got to run, Claudine. See you tonight." Miss Claudine waved to him as he left the studio.

As the class was emptying, Mr. and Mrs. Guthrie rushed over to their daughter. "You were wonderful, darling," Mrs. Guthrie said, giving Emma a hug. "Wonderful!"

"Very impressive," said her father.

"What about Charlie and Lindsey?" Emma asked, nodding at her friends who stood beside her. "They were good, too, weren't they?"

"You were all just wonderful!" Mrs. Guthrie agreed.

"We were just kind of the corps de ballet, as Miss Claudine would say. We were the background," said Charlie modestly.

"Emma was the real star," added Lindsey.

Miss Claudine came over and placed her hand on Emma's shoulder. She was very serious as she faced Mr. and Mrs. Guthrie. "I hope you will forgive me," she said.

"Why? What for?" asked Mrs. Guthrie.

"I almost made a tragic mistake by putting Emma on pointe," Miss Claudine told them, shaking her head sadly as she spoke. "Today I saw what truly great potential Emma has. By putting her on pointe I risk straining her ankles, maybe even her legs. To push such a great talent to flower before her time would be criminal. A great waste. I cannot afford to ruin the ankles of a genius."

Mrs. Guthrie looked horrified. "Of course not. That would be terrible."

"I knew you would understand," said Miss Claudine solemnly. "I must forbid Emma to go on pointe for at least another two years."

"Are you sure?" asked Mr. Guthrie. "She seemed pretty good to me today."

"Absolutely sure," said Miss Claudine. "You must trust me on this. Emma is so talented that I tried to push her, but it was a mistake."

"We'll trust your judgment," said Mrs. Guthrie. "We wouldn't want Emma's career ruined prematurely."

"All right, Emma?" asked Miss Claudine. "No

more toe shoes for at least two years. Do you think you can live with that?"

That was the best news Emma had heard all week. She smiled brightly—and then remembered that she was supposed to be disappointed. She quickly hung her head. "I suppose you know best, Miss Claudine," she said, trying to sound as sad as possible.

Charlie and Lindsey rolled their eyes and then ran ahead to the dressing room. Emma walked slowly out of the studio with her parents. "Are you very disappointed by what Miss Claudine said?" asked her father.

"Just a little," said Emma.

"You know, I noticed you've been walking funny lately," said her mother. "You're even limping a little now. Maybe it is for the best that you wait."

"I guess so," agreed Emma glumly, playing on her parents' sympathy for all it was worth.

"Go get changed and we'll talk some more over lunch," suggested her father.

"Okay!" Emma shouted happily and hurried off toward the dressing room. Inside she was greeted by Charlie and Lindsey, who were jumping up and down, squealing with delight.

"It was great! Better than we expected," said Charlie. All at once they sensed an icy glare boring into them. They turned and saw Danielle scowling at them from the corner of the room. Oddly enough, none of them felt like rubbing it in. Danielle didn't seem very important anymore. The important thing was that their performance had been a success.

"Do you think Miss Claudine meant that stuff about your great future?" asked Lindsey.

"Naw," said Emma.

"I don't know," Charlie said. "You never can tell with Miss Claudine."

Chapter Nine

"Are you strapped in back there?" asked Mr. Guthrie from the front seat of Mrs. Guthrie's green Jaguar.

"I am now," Emma answered, buckling her seat belt. Emma hadn't been in the backseat of this car for a long time—not since her parents divorced and the three of them stopped going places together. Though she knew it was just for the day, it was nice being together again as a family.

Mrs. Guthrie started the car and pulled out of the Eastbridge Mall parking lot. "That Miss Claudine is really quite nice," said Mrs. Guthrie at an intersection while they were waiting for the light to change.

"Yeah, she's pretty neat," Emma agreed.

"We talked to her while you were inside getting changed," said Mr. Guthrie. "She told us that you had put yourself through great pains to make this performance come out well. She said it was important to you to make us proud."

"She said that?" asked Emma, feeling slightly embarrassed.

"Mmmm, she did," said her mother, proceeding through the intersection when the light changed. "Emma, can I ask you something?"

"Sure."

"Have you been feeling neglected lately?"

Emma wasn't prepared for such a direct question. "Why are you asking?"

"Because Miss Claudine kept stressing how much our being at class today meant to you," her mother explained.

"We got the feeling that perhaps she was trying to give us a hint," her father added.

"Promise you won't get mad if I tell the truth?" Emma asked, not sure she really wanted to spoil this nice moment of togetherness with too much unpleasant truth telling.

Emma saw her parents look at one another with uncertain expressions, as if they wanted to say, "No, keep the truth to yourself." Then her father turned around in his seat to face her. "You have to tell us what you feel."

"Well," Emma began. "It used to be just Daddy who was always busy with work. Now you work full-time, Mom—so *both* of you are always busy with work."

"We have to work, Emma," said her mother.

"I know, but do you have to work every second of every day?" Emma exploded, feeling all her anger and unhappiness spilling out. "Sometimes I feel like I'm just this pain in the neck you have to put up with. Like I'm this big inconvenience."

Mrs. Guthrie turned the car off the busy road onto

a quiet residential street and pulled over to the curb. "Emma, that's awful," she said. "You honestly feel that way?"

"Sometimes," Emma admitted, unbuckling her seat belt and leaning forward between her parents. "I have to tell you something else, too. Miss Claudine didn't choose me to go on pointe. I tried to put myself on pointe so that both of you would be impressed with how talented I am. Miss Claudine was just covering up for me because I begged her to."

Mrs. Guthrie reached back and gently pushed some strands of hair from Emma's face. "I'm so sorry, Emma," she said. "I *have* been very wrapped up in my business, I know that. But you always seem so busy. I didn't think it bothered you."

"I don't want you to sit and stare at me all day," said Emma defensively.

"Just once in a while," suggested her mother.

"Yeah," Emma said shyly. "Like the other night when you were showing me your pictures. I liked that."

"Then we'll do more of it," her mother assured her. "I just never realized you felt like this."

"I'm glad that's settled," said Mr. Guthrie.

Emma and her mother turned to him with their jaws dropped in exaggerated expressions of shock. "Not so fast, buster," said Mrs. Guthrie.

"Daddy! You're worse than Mom!" Emma cried at the same time. "You only get to see me once a week and you don't even show up half the time."

Mr. Guthrie's eyes darted from his ex-wife to his daughter as though he felt trapped. "You're right," he said after an uncomfortable minute. "I guess I'm not used to having to set aside special time for my little girl. I just assume you're always going to be around, so if I don't see you this weekend, I'll catch you the next time."

"I miss you, though, Daddy," Emma said quietly. "When you don't show up I worry that maybe you're forgetting about me."

"Forget about . . . ? Oh, Emma, sweetheart, how could I ever forget about you?"

Emma looked at him with a doubting expression. "All right," he said. "I do see how you could get that impression. I was thoughtless, but it doesn't mean I don't love you. I'll do better in the future. I promise."

"Me, too," said Mrs. Guthrie.

"You'll still love me even if I'm not a great ballerina?" Emma asked timidly.

Mrs. Guthrie reached back and hugged Emma. "We love you, no matter what."

They decided to skip lunch at the diner, and went back to the house instead. Mr. Guthrie didn't seem to be in his usual rush to get back to the city. The three of them sat in the kitchen and ate sandwiches. Mr. Guthrie told them jokes he'd heard in the office. One of them struck Mrs. Guthrie as being so funny that tears of laughter rolled down her cheeks.

Emma smiled. It was so good to sit around and laugh together like they used to. "Emma, have you got any new drawings to show me?" her father asked.

Emma thought a moment. She got up and ran to her room, and returned with the drawings she'd done with her toes. "Very modern," said her father, squinting at the quivery lines. Emma explained how she'd drawn them with her feet to strengthen her toes.

"Who suggested that?" Mr. Guthrie asked, impressed.

"Nobody," Emma told him proudly. "I thought of it myself."

"That's our Emma," said Mrs. Guthrie.

"Always thinking," added Mr. Guthrie.

"I *am* always thinking, aren't I?" Emma said, glad that they realized she was clever. "Sometimes I just can't stop."

"You get that from me," said Mr. and Mrs. Guthrie, speaking at the same time. The three of them looked at one another and then burst out laughing.

When lunch was over, Mr. Guthrie got up from the table. "I'll come get you next Saturday night and we'll spend all Sunday in the city together," he promised. Emma hugged him and walked him to the front door.

She'd just closed the door when the bell rang. It was Charlie and Lindsey. They all smiled at each other as if they shared a secret, and Emma led them into the living room. "How are your feet?" Charlie asked, making herself comfortable on the leather sofa.

"Horrible. They're killing me," Emma said dramatically.

"You sure look happy for someone with horrible feet," Lindsey observed, settling down on the rug.

Emma shrugged. "I'm a very complex person," she said with a grin.

"Listen, complex person," said Mrs. Guthrie as she came into the room, "how would you like it if I drove

90

you and your pals here down to Johnson's for some banana splits to celebrate your performance today?"

"Cool!" Emma cried.

"Get your coats on and we'll go," said Mrs. Guthrie. As she spoke, the phone rang. "Just one second," she said, picking it up. "Hello," she spoke to the person on the other end. "No, it's fine to call on a Saturday. I don't mind at all. You're interested in signing a contract? That's wonderful! Yes, we can discuss it right now. It's no problem, I was just—" Mrs. Guthrie stopped herself and looked at Emma's disappointed face. "Actually, I was just taking my daughter out. Can I call you back on Monday? Sorry, but now isn't a good time." Mrs. Guthrie hung up the phone.

"Thanks, Mom," said Emma.

Her mother nodded and smiled. "Let's go," she said.

Outside, Charlie and Lindsey raced one another to the car. "Hurry up," they called to Emma, who limped along behind them. They ran back to her and, grasping one another's wrists, they made a seat with their hands.

"Sit back and relax," said Lindsey cheerfully. "You deserve a break."

Giggling, Emma let them carry her to the car. "Make way for Mademoiselle Emma!" cried Charlie. "She suffered, but she was great!"

Emma and Charlie are all excited about the dazzling new costumes that Miss Claudine has ordered for the big dance recital. But Lindsey has a secret problem, and she's afraid she won't be able to perform. Can her friends help her in a pinch? Don't miss their grand finale in *Three for the Show*, book #6 in the NO WAY BALLET series!